HAM-HUGS
ALL AROUND

Adapted by Ruth Koeppel
Illustrated by Steve Haefele

ISBN 0-439-56115-9

HAMTARO ® or ™, the Hamtaro logo, and all related characters and elements are trademarks of Shogakukan Production Co., Ltd.

© R. KAWAI / 2000, 2003 Shogakukan, SMDE, TV Tokyo. All Rights Reserved.

Published by Scholastic Inc.
SCHOLASTIC and associated logos are trademarks and/or registered trademarks of Scholastic Inc.

Design by Peter Koblish

12 11 10 9 8 7 6 5 4 3 2 1
4 5 6 7 8/0

Printed in the U.S.A.
First printing, January 2004

SCHOLASTIC INC.
New York   Toronto   London   Auckland   Sydney
Mexico City   New Delhi   Hong Kong   Buenos Aires

"It's almost Valentine's Day!" said Pashmina. "Bijou, what are you giving everyone?"
"I was thinking tuna tarts and carrot cupcakes," replied Bijou.
"Yum," said Sandy. "That sounds delicious."

"Sandy, what are you giving Maxwell?" asked Bijou.
"I haven't decided yet," Sandy said with a secret smile.
Pashmina rolled her eyes. "He'll like whatever you give him."

Hamtaro and Oxnard raced back to the clubhouse. "The girls are making Valentine's Day gifts for us!" shouted Hamtaro.
"Valentine's Day gifts?" asked Boss. "What for?"
"To show how much they like us," said Hamtaro.

"We'd better get busy thinking of something for them!"
said Hamtaro. "Hmm . . . what would the girls really like?"
"I know—sunflower seeds!" shouted Oxnard.
"No, that won't do," said Hamtaro. "It should be something
special we make ourselves."

The boys came up with some ideas and got started. They worked well alongside one another—at least at first.

"Hey, Boss, do you mind if I borrow some glue?" Maxwell asked.

"I was thinking I'd make Sandy—"

"Gather your own supplies!" Boss thundered.

Then Howdy and Dexter started fighting over the last piece of red construction paper.
"I need this paper to finish Pashmina's gift," said Dexter.
"So do I," said Howdy. "Besides Pashmina likes me better."
"No she doesn't!" shouted Dexter. "Take that back!"

"There must be an easier way to get ready for Valentine's Day,"
said Hamtaro. "Let's see if the girls are having any better luck."
The boys couldn't quite see what the girls were making.
But one thing was for sure—the girls were working together.
"Why didn't we think of that?" asked Hamtaro.

Once they returned to the clubhouse the boys quickly got back to work.

"Your present for Bijou looks great," said Maxwell.

"Thanks," said Boss. "Do you need some more glue?"

"The girls are going to love our Valentine's Day gifts," said Hamtaro as he divided the construction paper between Howdy and Dexter.

Bright and early on Valentine's Day morning the boys paid the girls a visit. Hamtaro showered the girls with confetti. Boss gave Bijou his handmade valentine.
"Ooh, la, la, you are so sweet," said Bijou.

Howdy and Dexter each handed Pashmina a paper flower. "Both of these flowers are beautiful," said Pashmina. Maxwell gave Sandy a paper chain for jumping rope. Sandy gave Maxwell a ham-hug. It was the best present he ever got.

The girls surprised the boys with a box of chestnuts. Oxnard couldn't resist grabbing one. "Chestnuts are my favorite!" he said. "After sunflower seeds, that is."

The Ham-Hams sat down and shared their holiday feast. "Hip-ham hooray for Valentine's Day!" everyone cheered.